# THE PALACE HOTEL

## A SHORT STORY

### ALEXANDRIA BLAELOCK

BlueMere Books
MELBOURNE, AUSTRALIA

For permission requests, please contact
enquiries@bluemerebooks.com.

Ordering Information:
Discounts are available on quantity purchases. For details, contact orders@bluemerebooks.com.

The Palace Hotel/Alexandria Blaelock
paperback ISBN: 978-1-922744-04-3
digital ISBN: 978-1-922744-05-0

# THE PALACE HOTEL

Diana closed her eyes and rested her cheek on the roughhewn table. Maybe not the wisest thing to do because it did give her the look of someone who'd drunk too much and passed out.

But really, she hadn't got started yet.

She'd loosely tied her red hair up, and was enjoying the warmth of the morning sun on the back of her exposed neck and the light scent of sun warmed flowers while she listened to cockatoos screeching in the distance.

Screeching; the soundtrack of her life.

If not the birds, then her mother, her brother, sister-in-law, sister, brother-in-law.

Her ex-husband. The other ex-husband.

The dog.

Though he whined more than screeched, and that was mostly okay.

She reached a hand under the table to scratch the top of his ageing Labrador head. He licked her bare leg in reply, and rested his head on her foot.

No way to tell whether her father was a screecher, he'd disappeared when she was only a year or two old.

Popped down to the milk bar for a packet of fags and never seen or heard of again.

Good riddance according to her mother, but as it turned out, you could take anything she said with a kilo or two of salt.

More likely he saw the way the future was shaping up and got out while he still could.

Footsteps approached, and she sat up trying not to look as exhausted as she felt.

The pretty young girl smiled and placed her large latte on the table, complementary biscuit resting in the saucer. "Your burger's on the way."

Diana nodded her thanks and reached for the coffee.

She held the glass in both hands and took a moment to inhale the intoxicating aroma. Hopefully it would be good.

It was generally possible to get a decent cup most places, but some of the roadhouses could still be a bit hit and miss.

This roadhouse sat in the top of a Y junction; all you could see as you looked down any of the three roads was a distant shimmering heat haze spreading out across the vast ocean of red outback desert.

It looked positively civilised from the outside. In the middle, a large, well maintained parking lot interspersed with ghost gums and desert oaks providing a small amount of shade.

On one arm, the covered petrol and diesel pumps backed onto a flat, miraculously green grassy area sprinkled with picnic settings and a couple of gas barbecues.

She'd driven in at dawn, and after climbing out of the car, spent endless minutes spellbound by a mob of kangaroos quietly grazing on the dew speckled grass. The odd ear twitch almost the only movement.

The modern ablution block was absolutely delightful with spotless toilet and shower facilities, good strong water pressure and lots of unmetered steaming hot water.

Her long hot shower had probably used more water than was wise for a desert installation, but she'd needed it.

And even better, the fresh, citrus scented soap bars in the vending machine didn't draw all the moisture from her skin.

On the other arm, stood a small, but neat and trim red brick hotel complex, its Palace Hotel sign faded and barely legible.

And at the back, a long cafe come general and souvenir store with an enclosed outdoor, dog-friendly eating area attached.

In which she and Oscar currently sat.

If she'd suddenly woken to find herself in this magical courtyard, she'd have thought it was a small wedding chapel garden not a country roadhouse in the middle of nowhere.

The large folding glass doors from the cafe were currently open to let the slight breeze through.

On two sides, the tall red brick walls hosted fragrant white jasmine growing up wires anchored to the bricks.

In the garden beds around the edges, ragged lavenders and rosemary grew.

And all around, in the beds and coming up between the matching red brick pavers, there were small pastel pink and purple daisies.

Bees droned between the flowers and butterflies drifted above.

The fourth wall framed a view of the parking lot through surprisingly elaborate ironwork gates.

Even though she'd entered through the gates, and could clearly see the parking lot, she had the feeling that when she walked back out of them, she'd find herself in a different world entirely.

Which was a bit disconcerting seeing as you couldn't take dogs through the cafe.

Diana shrugged one shoulder and took a sip of coffee.

It was just the right blend of strong coffee and rich, sweet, creamy milk.

Wherever she ended up, at least she'd be with Oscar. Who twitched in his sleep and farted.

The coffee's perfection seemed to suggest that regardless of what anyone else thought, she was heading in the right direction.

Even though she had no idea where she was going, when she'd get there, or what she'd find.

Except maybe a bed more comfortable than the back seat of her red vintage Chrysler Valiant Charger.

Still cupping the tall glass in both hands, she drank half of it while it was still hot enough to burn her throat slightly all the way down.

It was good.

Not for the first time, she wondered what possessed her to her quit her job, sell off the bulk of her possessions and hit the road.

Nothing to tie her down or call her back.

Not that her job, flat or family were anything much to write home about, but other people seemed perfectly content with these small things in their small ordinary lives.

What was it about her that set her on the road searching for something else?

Some nameless thing she felt she'd lost.

Following in her father's footsteps no doubt.

Oscar stirred as the girl brought the burger, "You can pay inside when you're done."

Diana flipped the lid off, and ate the beetroot followed by the pineapple slice, tomato and onion rings. She put the lid back on and cut the burger in half, making sure she cut through the egg so the yolk poured over the bacon and pooled on the plate with the sauce.

Then she dropped half on the ground for the dog and neatly nibbled her way through the other, dipping it in the egg yolk now and then.

It was delicious, like the coffee.

Possibly the best she'd ever eaten.

Why is it that food in the Country is always tastier and more real than food in the City?

She licked her fingers, and seeing as no one was looking, slipped over to the dog water fountain to wash her hands under the running water.

Oscar padded over to take a drink.

As she finished her coffee, he leaned, nodding, on her legs.

Poor old Oscar.

He was getting to old for travel now, he really needed a nice quiet place in the sunshine for good long bone warming naps.

"Stay," she told him as she stood to go inside and pay.

He slid to the ground and sniffed at it, as if that was exactly what he had been hoping to do.

Next to the register, was a large, handwritten sign.

HELP WANTED

So of course she asked what help, and the girl sent her out the back to the office to see Gary.

Who was an older guy, his greying hair pulled back in a bun held in place by a pen.

It gave him the look of a man who should be out speeding down the highway on a Hog, not sitting behind a desk driving a computer, cussing with mouse rage.

Diana knocked on the door frame startling him into a different kind of cussing rage.

"Don't sneak up on me, he gasped, "I'm an old man, you'll give me a heart attack."

"I'm sorry, it's about the help wanted sign out the front?"

"Ah, the help is to replace me."

Diana frowned and scratched her head, "you're looking for a recruitment consultant?"

He laughed, "No. I guess I didn't explain that well. I'm looking for a Hotel Manager to take over from me.

"You don't have to worry about the big stuff, that's all taken care of by the Big Guy down

South. Just the day-to-day running of the place - making sure it's clean and tidy, and ordering the stock. Some handyman work."

"I was an Office Manager for a time. Is it like that, only bigger?"

"Almost exactly like that. When can you start?"

"Don't you want any references or anything?"

"No, the Big Guy told me someone was on the way and to hire the first person who asked."

Diana frowned again. It sounded like she was about to become the front person for a money laundering/drug smuggling/prostitution racket.

"Gary, is there something illegal about this place?"

"Not at all. The owner was in a hunting accident years ago and has been in a coma ever since. The Big Guy takes care of all his personal stuff, and I just take care of the local roadhouse and hotel specific things.

"The worst you'll come up against is his hunting buddies monthly meet-up. Some of their ceremonial garb is completely nuts: horned heads, coats of leaves and stuff. Nuts, but all above board. Completely legit."

"Sounds fascinating."

"Yeah, but don't get excited, you don't get to go to the meetings and they lock the doors so you can't get in while they're there," he replied.

"Ah. An Ancient Secret Society. I can manage that."

"I'd be more worried by the invisible cleaning staff. I pay their wages, but I never see them."

Diana laughed, "just as well they're doing an excellent job then."

"True enough."

"I guess I could take care of that, but what if something goes wrong?"

"You just email the Big Guy and he takes care of it."

Diana didn't have any plans - staying was as good an option as getting back in the car and driving away.

In fact, thinking of Oscar, potentially a better option.

And a regular income might come in handy.

What was the worst that could happen, she wondered.

Dying was unlikely, raped and beaten up slightly more likely, but she was quick on her feet and had some Aikido training.

She wouldn't own the roadhouse, so her personal liability would probably be limited to operating within the law.

Gary seemed to think the business was all legitimate, so little chance of being caught up in a Police sting.

She couldn't stop the words coming out of her mouth, "Okay, I'll do it."

And while she should have been freaked out by taking a job with no mention of pay or conditions, the thought didn't occur to her.

All she really thought about, was the pleasure of staying in one place for a while.

That she could have stopped moving at any time, and in fact hadn't wanted to stop moving until five minutes ago, didn't cross her mind.

"That's great news!

"Salary is $65,000, plus hotel accommodation with a small private yard."

"Fine," she was relieved she wouldn't have to find somewhere to live nearby.

And very handy that there was a place within walking distance that made the best burgers!

"Oh! There is just one thing. You have to have a hunting dog. Do you have a hunting dog?"

"A hunting dog? That seems a weird kind of screening criteria."

"I know, but it's what the Big Guy wanted. Maybe it's so's the hunting buddies are comfortable. Or as a guard dog more likely."

"Well, I have a dog, and he's a hunting breed, but I think his hunting days are behind him."

"Good enough. The job's yours." Gary moved some stacks of papers around on his desk and dragged out a folder, which he tipped out on the top.

He shuffled a few pages around, pulled the pen out from his hair, and offered it to her.

"Sign here to accept the job offer." She scanned through the terms and conditions which seemed in order so she signed it.

"Sign this indemnity for claims, damages or liabilities brought against you in your capacity as Hotel Manager." Similarly fine.

"Fill out your bank account and superannuation details here for your salary payments." Duly taken care of.

He shuffled the papers, loaded them into an ancient fax machine, and tapped in the number.

The machine screeched and burbled, and after a little while it beeped to indicate it was done.

A moment later it spat out a receipt indicating a successful send.

Gary nodded, then picked up an old leather pair of saddlebags and starting filling them up with bits and pieces from around the office.

When he was done packing, he threw the bag over his shoulder, and smiled warmly at her.

He held out his hand to shake, "Good luck, though I'm sure you won't need it."

Diana shook the proffered hand and trailed behind him as he strode from the office, taller, straighter and younger than he'd seemed when she walked in.

He stopped by the cash register, "Everyone, can I have your attention please?"

A couple of people appeared from the kitchen.

"This is Diana, she'll be taking over from me, and I know you'll treat her as well as you've treated me.

"It's been great knowing you, but now it's time for me to move on. I wish you all the best for your futures."

Diana frowned as she watched the three of them cluster around Gary, shaking his hand and wishing him well.

She'd expected he'd tell her to start Monday, but it looked like he was about to walk out and not come back.

No handover, no instruction, no nothing.

Moments later, she was chasing him from the cafe, "But what do I do?"

"Same thing you'd do anywhere else, there's nothing much different here to any other place."

"But what about your systems and passwords and things?"

"The Big Guy will fax you what you need to know, and you'll change everything I've done anyway."

"But, where do I start?"

She ran into him as he stopped next to a sky-blue Harley-Davidson in the motorcycle parking, and started tying the bags on it.

"Look, you don't need to worry about anything, this place runs itself.

"You can do as much or as little as you're comfortable with. You're really just here to make the ordinary suburban people comfortable - you give them a face to put on things they don't understand, like green grass in the desert."

"But—"

"I know this seems like madness, but it doesn't matter what I tell you. When you walk back in there, it will be a different roadhouse.

"It will be your place, with your rules - my rules don't apply."

"But—"

"It's too late," he smiled, "you signed the papers, and you have to go back in for Oscar."

"Wait a minute, I never told you his name."

His smile widened, "I told you, the Big Guy said you were coming."

He rested one hand on her shoulder and leaned down to meet her eyes, "You really don't need to worry about anything.

"You *are* in the right place. Everything *is* as it should be. You *don't* need me."

And then he swung his right leg over the bike, started the engine, put the kick stand up and rode away.

Holding her hand to her forehead as a sunshade, she watched him shrink and disappear into the heat haze before she turned to look back at the roadhouse.

Which looked exactly the same, aside from Oscar and three staff standing in the courtyard behind the ornate gates watching her.

Creepily like the servants lined up to welcome the new master in some kind of period drama.

The gate was enticingly ajar, and she was sure she'd closed it behind her when she first walked through it only an hour or two ago.

The courtyard seen through the gates seemed slightly blurry, with random sparkly lights twinkling.

The kind you often see when you get a migraine.

It had all seemed perfectly normal five minutes ago, but now, it was somehow mystical and mysterious.

She'd got it wrong - the different world wasn't out here, it was back in there.

If she walked back in there, nothing would be the same again.

But Gary said this was her fate.

Well, that's not exactly what he'd said.

What he'd said was that she was in the right place, it was just that she'd understood it as something else.

Was this the thing that was missing from her life?

She had the feeling the roadhouse car park was a crinkle in reality as she knew it.

She could step forward into some other kind of universe, or backwards into the world she knew. Either way there would be no coming back.

All in.

She reminded herself, she had nothing to lose.

Except maybe Oscar.

Who seemed to have made his own decision as he lay down with a grunt and a thump.

She hesitated a moment longer.

Then she straightened her spine and tried to look commanding, which is not easy for a girl in ragged cut off denim shorts and a long tank top.

As she took her first step towards the waiting staff, a gust of wind blew up, pulling her hair loose from its ties and setting it dancing around her face like an electric orange halo.

**THE END**

# ABOUT THE AUTHOR

Alexandria Blaelock writes stories, some of them for *Ellery Queen's Mystery Magazine* and *Pulphouse Fiction Magazine*. She's also written five self-help books applying business techniques to personal matters like getting dressed, cleaning house, and feeding your friends.

As a recovering Project Manager, she's probably too fond of sticking to plan. She lives in a forest because she enjoys birdsong, the scent of gum leaves and the sun on her face. When not telecommuting to parallel universes from her Melbourne based imagination, she watches K-dramas, talks to animals, and drinks Campari. At the same time.

Discover more at www.alexandriablaelock.com.

# BOOKS BY
# ALEXANDRIA BLAELOCK

## SHORT STORY COLLECTIONS

The Histories of Hayward Hall
Lovelorn, Lovestruck and Love at First Sight
Common or Garden Variety Heroes
Case Files of the Wilkinson Detective Agency
Unavoidable Fates
Christmas Travesties

## OTHER FICTION

That Love Nonsense

## MS BLAELOCK'S BOOKS

Stress Free Dinner Parties
Signature Wardrobe Planning
Holistic Personal Finance
Minimally Viable Housekeeping
Planning a Life Worth Living

# SELECTED SHORT STORIES

Alma's Grace
Balancing the Book
Carmelita Basingstoke
Fate in Your Hands
Kiss of Death
Lady of the Looking Glass
Life in the Security Directorate
Long Weekend in the Snow
Love in the Past Tense
Love in the Security Directorate
Morning Star, Evening Star, Superstar
Needy Bitch
Payton's Run
Phoenix Child
Secret Singer
Shining Star
Ship in a Bottle
Simone Says Hands in the Air
Special Relativity in Space
The Bygone Boyfriend
The Day the Schedule Broke
The Ghost Detectors
The Guardian's Vigil
The Mince Pie Mystery
The Mystery of the Master Suite
The Pseudonym's Bride
The Shadow Thieves
The Time-Space Paradox
Toy Soldiers